for lots of things.

For Mommy

Lots of Thanks!

A little book about being thankful

Illustrated by Thierry Courtin

I give lots of thanks

and Daddy.

For hugs

and kisses.

For friends

and more friends!

For music.

But most of all . . .

I give lots of thanks

for things that make me happy!

$4.99 US
($7.50 CAN)

Babies give lots of thanks for lots of things . . . for Mommy and Daddy, for hugs and for kisses. Here, for the youngest of readers, is an introduction to being thankful.

What are you thankful for?

ISBN 0-448-42623-4 A B C D E F G H I J

ISBN 0-448-42623-4
EAN
9 780448 426235
90000>